Say peekaboo!

Bunny's Best Valentine

Anne Forni

Sébastien Braun

DK

It's **Valentine's Day** tomorrow
and the Peekaboo animals
are all very busy.

I wonder what they are doing?

Chick has been secretly making a Valentine card for her best friend, Bunny.

"I love **Valentine's Day**! I'm making a card for Bunny. He will be surprised."

The Valentine card is ready, so Chick licks
and sticks down the envelope flap.

"I'll run and hide it in Bunny's letterbox."

Chick hurries along the path
towards Bunny's burrow.

"I wonder if anyone will
send me a Valentine
card this year..."

On her way Chick passes the rocky heap where Kid loves to climb. But today Kid is busy doing something else…

"Peekaboo!"

calls Chick, popping her head up over the rocks.

Kid is surprised to see her.

"What are you doing with those ribbons, Kid?" asks Chick.

"It's a **secret!**" says Kid, as he tries to hide the ribbons.

"**Most mysterious!**" thinks Chick and on she runs, with Bunny's Valentine card safely tucked under her wing.

At the pond, Chick spots her friend Duck, who is busy stirring something in a mixing bowl.

"Peekaboo!"

calls Chick, jumping out
from the reeds.

Duck is surprised to see Chick.
"What are you making?" asks Chick.

"It's a **secret!**" says Duck
and she pushes the bowl
and spoon out of sight.

"**Most mysterious!**"
thinks Chick, and on she
runs, still holding tight to
Bunny's Valentine card.

Over by the hedge Chick sees
Squirrel, who is busy sewing.
"Peekaboo!" calls Chick,
popping her head up over the leaves.

"What are
you making?"
asks Chick.

"...it's a **secret!**" says Squirrel, hiding the sewing machine with his bushy tail.

"**Most mysterious!**" thinks Chick and on she runs towards Bunny's burrow. "I wonder why everyone is so busy today... and so secretive."

Down the lane, Fox and Foal are carrying something.

They see Chick coming and try to hide, but Chick **spots them**.

“Peekaboo!”

says Chick.

“What are you carrying?
Where are you going?”

"Nothing..." says Foal.

"Nowhere..." says Fox.

"It must be something. Let me see!" says Chick.

"No! It's a **secret!**" say Fox and Foal together.

"**Most mysterious!**" says Chick and on she runs towards Bunny's burrow.

Across the field Chick sees Lamb, who is very busy making something.

"Peekaboo!"

"What are you doing?" she asks.

“It’s a **secret!**” says Lamb, and she turns her head away from Chick.

“**Most mysterious!** I wonder why everybody is being so secretive today,” says Chick.

“Phew! I’m nearly at Bunny’s burrow. I hope he isn’t at home, so I can hide his card…”

Chick creeps towards Bunny's letterbox to post the card, when out comes Bunny.

“Peekaboo!”

says Bunny, quickly hiding something.
“What are you up to?”

“Nothing!” says Chick.
“Just passing by...”

"Well, I must dash, Chick. Very busy today!" And Bunny speeds away.

"I wonder where he is going in such a hurry?" says Chick. "**Most mysterious!**"

Chick pops Bunny's card
into the letterbox.

"Bunny will find it in the morning. It will be
a lovely **Valentine's Day** surprise for him."

That night the
Peekaboo animals dream
about **Valentine's Day**...

...and Chick dreams
about Bunny
opening his card.

The next morning it's **Valentine's Day**.
Chick comes out from her hen house
and, what a **big surprise!** It looks
like there is going to be a party!

The decorations her friends have made are everywhere. There is tasty food on the table and there, right in the middle, is a large pink envelope with Chick's name on it.

"But **where is everyone?**" asks Chick.

“Peek

aboo!”

Bunny opens the card Chick had hidden in his letterbox.

Chick picks up her card from the table and opens it.

"But **who is it from**...?" they both wonder.

"It's a secret!"

"Happy Valentine's Day, everybody!"

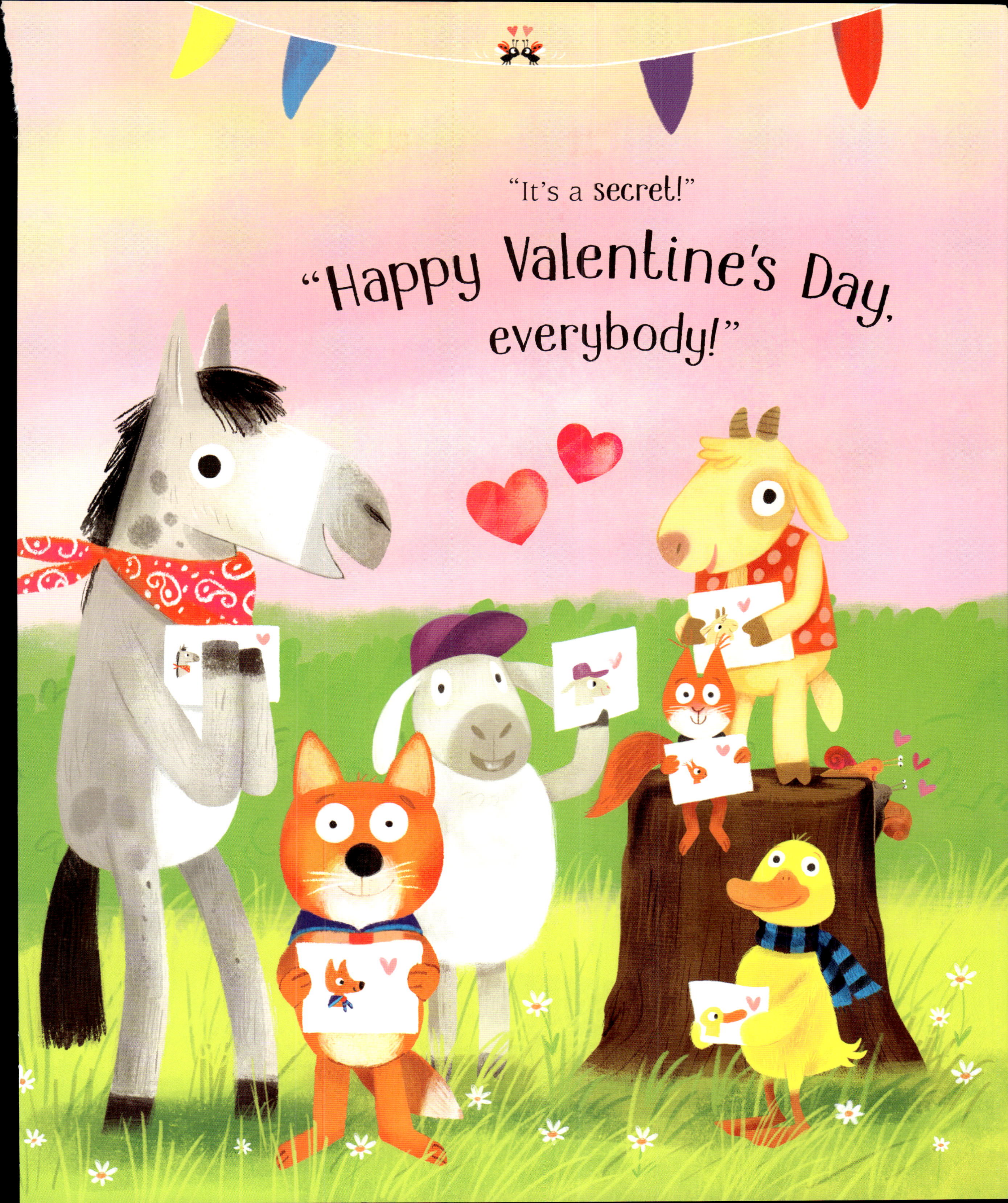

DK | Penguin Random House

Author Anne Forni
Illustrator Sébastien Braun

First published in Great Britain in 2025 by Dorling Kindersley Limited
20 Vauxhall Bridge Road, London SW1V 2SA

The authorised representative in the EEA is
Dorling Kindersley Verlag GmbH. Arnulfstr. 124, 80636 Munich, Germany

10 9 8 7 6 5 4 3 2 1
001–351042–Nov/2025

A CIP catalogue record for this book is available from the British Library.
ISBN: 978-0-2417-5837-3

Printed and bound in China

www.dk.com

FSC www.fsc.org MIX Paper | Supporting responsible forestry FSC™ C018179

This book was made with Forest Stewardship Council™ certified paper – one small step in DK's commitment to a sustainable future.
Learn more at www.dk.com/uk/information/sustainability